Dark Brandon and the Evil King Con

A Children's Tale for Freedom-Loving Adults

Written by L.B. Tee

Illustrated by C.M. Bohld

Dark Brandon and the Evil King Con was published with simple language and whimsical illustrations to explain why the November 5, 2024 presidential election is one of the most important in U.S. history and to help get out the vote. The author was not authorized, influenced, nor paid by a political candidate nor a committee controlled by a political candidate.

Virginia Beach-Norfolk-Newport News, VA-NC Metropolitan Area

Identifiers: ISBN 978-1-7334054-2-3 (paperback)
ISBN 978-1-7334054-3-0 (e-book)

Library of Congress Control Number: 2024906545

To freedom-loving people everywhere

Land of the Free
RULED BY THE PEOPLE
DEMOCRACY
USA CONSTITUTION
FOR THE PEOPLE

Once upon a time there was a free and fabulous country called the United States of America. The USA was a democracy. This means America was ruled by its citizens through fair elections of some citizens to represent all in the country's government.

The rules for protecting the people's rights and freedoms and for running the country were written in a very important official paper called the Constitution.

For over 200 years this fabulous country's democracy and its Constitution served its people well.

Then one day a rich and famous man decided America wasn't fabulous anymore and that only he could make it fabulous again. He also didn't like the country's Constitution. His name was Mr. Imah Con.

Mr. Con lived a life fit for a king with a private jet and a home with gold walls, gold ceilings, and gold chandeliers. Even though he lived like a king, Imah Con had quite a few failed businesses and owed the banks a lot of money.

Other people lost their own money in his failed businesses. But he had one very important talent. He knew how to make people believe he was a big success.

He got himself on TV and radio and in newspapers
bragging that he was a big success. He hired writers to write
books that looked like he wrote them so he could brag
some more about his big success.

And because everybody thought he was a big success
somebody gave him his own TV show where he could act
like he was a big success. This made him even more famous.

Mr. Con figured since people believed he was a big success
he'd also get them to believe he could save them from all
their troubles. So he started a club called Make America
Fabulous Again, and he attracted millions of MAFA
members.

MAFA
CON
MAFA
MAFA
MAFA
MAFA
MAFA
MAFA
MAFA
MAKE
AMERICA
FABULOUS
AGAIN

Imah Con claimed he was the only one that cared about his MAFA followers, that everyone else was their enemy, that real Americans would be replaced with immigrants.

He told his followers all they had to do for him to save them was to vote to make him president of the USA. And so they did. He became President Imah Con, leader of the greatest country in the world.

While he was president he didn't fix anyone's troubles. He didn't make the country any more fabulous than it was before. But he did help the rich get richer and the poor get poorer.

Many American military men and women had died or were captured fighting for their country, but President Con called them losers.

When a terrible disease swept through the land President Con made believe it was nothing to worry about and let thousands of people die before he tried to protect them.

He became America's top role model for bullying, and lying, and name-calling, and temper tantrums, and attacking anyone who said anything he didn't like.

President Con stirred up much hatred and anger among the people of the country. Friends and family members turned against each other, fighting over whether he would save or destroy America.

President Con was responsible for rolling back women's rights, consumers' rights, workers' rights, voting rights, civil rights, human rights, climate change protections, and ignored the Constitution.

Yet, even after all this, his followers worshipped him. And when his years were almost up as president Imah Con asked the citizens of the USA to vote to make him president again.

But, this entire time there was a special man closely watching Imah Con, and he could not bear to watch anymore. His name was Dark Brandon.

Dark Brandon was not a rich man. But he was famous for living his whole life serving the American people to make their lives better. And for joining world leaders who sought global peace.

Those who knew him said he was a decent, wise man. He championed women's rights, consumers' rights, workers' rights, voting rights, civil rights, human rights, climate change protections, and defended the Constitution.

Dark Brandon decided he was the man for the job to beat
Ima Con for the presidency. He picked a smart vice-
president, and together they went up against President Con.
When election day came they won. By seven million votes.
The most votes a presidential team had won in United
States history.

Imah Con lost in a fair election. All the courts said it was
fair. All the states' election officers said it was fair. Even
many of his own people said it was fair.

But President Imah Con would not accept the results of the
fair election. He told his followers it was stolen from him.

Imah Con got his followers to try to keep him as president by leading them in a violent revolt at the US Capitol building. Many of his followers carried weapons. Police officers were killed, and many other police officers were injured by the mob. It was a very sad time in America.

However, the Imah Con Revolt to overturn the will of the people failed, and he had to leave.

On his way out Imah Con took hundreds of the government's top secret papers, including secrets on nuclear weapons. He hid them many miles away in his own house and tried to keep them when the government said he had to give them back.

Because the Imah Con Revolt failed, Dark Brandon became president and fulfilled his promises. Millions of good-paying jobs were created throughout the country. More people had jobs than ever before in America's history. Many more small businesses expanded or opened.

A new law created a USA manufacturing boom and also ensured future technologies would be American-made. New plants were started to make important parts and products, which before had been made overseas. Another law was passed to repair or replace the country's crumbling bridges and roads.

One more law helped remove guns from dangerous people, support school safety, and make communities safer. President Dark Brandon also appointed judges that reflected America's diversity.

Prices for several prescription drugs came down. Millions of people were able to get government health insurance, more than ever before. Student loan debt was reduced, and there were new investments in education. Actions were taken against unfair pricing and hidden fees by big businesses.

President Dark Brandon deployed more agents and officers for strong border security than any other president, and he led the way for the toughest, fairest border law in decades.

Plans for many new or expanded clean energy plants started due to the largest effort in fighting climate change in the country's history. President Dark Brandon rejoined an agreement with other nations in the global effort against climate change.

President Dark Brandon led other free countries in working to preserve democracies around the world…. But, democracy in the USA was soon to be threatened again.

Remember Imah Con? Even though he lost by seven million votes in a fair election for president, he kept lying that it was stolen from him. And his followers still believed him. He said he would run for president again and punish all his enemies.

Imah Con's followers continued to worship him because they thought he was the only one who could save them from all their troubles and make America fabulous again.

But Imah Con no longer wished to be just president. He craved much more than that. He planned to be King Con, tyrannical ruler of all. Once elected, he would erode citizens' rights that he reduced before as president -- only worse this time. And, charge people he didn't like with crimes.

He planned to release convicted rioters in the violent Imah Con Revolt at the US Capitol building. Use the military to squash peaceful demonstrations against him. Crack down on the free press so it wouldn't be free anymore.

To help himself get elected he secretly killed the country's tough, fair, border bill so he could make voters think only he could protect the border.

Dark Brandon's term as president was almost over.

Imah Con was preparing to rule the country with an iron fist. It was a scary time for America and everywhere else because the USA was the leader of the free world.

So President Dark Brandon decided he'd run for president against Imah Con a second time to keep the country free. And a great battle for democracy began. It was not a battle with guns or tanks, but a battle with the citizens' most powerful weapon: the right to vote.

Dark Brandon told the people they had a choice. They could vote for him and keep their democracy or they could vote for Imah Con and be ruled by an evil king.

It was more important than ever for the citizens to vote.

The big election day finally came. Millions more citizens voted than ever before. They knew there needed to be such a huge vote for democracy that it would never be threatened again.

As people poured into their voting places a new feeling of hope spread throughout the land. American citizens everywhere united to protect their country from tyranny.

In the end --- the winner was democracy! Dark Brandon won the presidency once again! The people danced in the streets and sang for joy that they had kept their country free.

So that was how Dark Brandon and the freedom-loving people of the USA beat the Evil King Con. And because America never took democracy for granted again, America stayed fabulous after all.

Vote early
or on Election Day
11-5-2024
for Biden/Harris

Protect
your
freedom

vote.gov
for voting
information

"Bad officials
are elected by
good citizens
who don't vote."
- George Jean Nathan

"Not voting is not
a protest.
It is a surrender."
- Keith Ellison

"WHEN YOU DON'T VOTE,
YOU'RE LETTING SOMEONE ELSE
TAKE POWER OVER YOUR OWN
LIFE."
- MICHELLE OBAMA

"The ballot is stronger than the bullet."
- Abraham Lincoln

"OUR LIVES BEGIN TO END THE DAY WE BECOME SILENT ABOUT THINGS THAT MATTER."
- MARTIN LUTHER KING, JR

"PEOPLE HAVE DIED FOR OUR FREEDOMS."
- SONYA SOTOMAYOR

"I'm hopeful that despite all the noise, all the lies, we're going to remember who we are, who we're called to be. Out of this political darkness, I see a great awakening. If you vote, things will get better, it will be a start."
- Barack Obama

"The future of this republic is in the hands of the American voter."
- Dwight D. Eisenhower

9 781733 405423